My 1st
Classic
Story

Tom Thumb

a retelling of the Grimm's fairy tale

by Eric Blair

illustrated by Todd Ouren

PICTURE WINDOW BOOKS

a capstone imprint

My First Classic Story is published by Picture Window Books
A Capstone Imprint
151 Good Counsel Drive, P.O. Box 669
Mankato, Minnesota 56002
www.capstonepub.com

Printed in the United States of America in North Mankato, Minnesota.
032010
005740CGF10

Library of Congress Cataloging-in-Publication data
Blair, Eric.
Tom Thumb : a retelling of the Grimms' fairy tale
retold by Eric Blair ; illustrated by Todd Ouren.
p. cm. — (My first classic story)
Summary: A boy the size of his father's thumb has a series of
adventures, including stopping a pair of thieves, being swallowed
by a cow, and tricking a wolf into bringing him back home.
ISBN 978-1-4048-6071-1 (library binding)
[1. Fairy tales. 2. Folklore—England.] I. Ouren, Todd, ill.
II. Grimm, Jacob, 1785-1863. III. Grimm, Wilhelm, 1786-1859.
IV. Tom Thumb. English. V. Title.
PZ8.B5688Tom 2011
398.2dc22
[E]   2010003627

Art Director: Kay Fraser
Graphic Designer: Emily Harris

The story of *Tom Thumb* has been passed down for generations. There are many versions of the story. The following tale is a retelling of the original version. While the story has been cut for length and level, the basic elements of the classic tale remain.

Once upon a time, there was a poor woodcutter who had no children.

"I'd love to have a child, even if he were as small as a thumb," he said.

4

Soon after, the woodcutter and his wife had a baby boy. He was no bigger than a thumb, so his parents named him Tom Thumb.

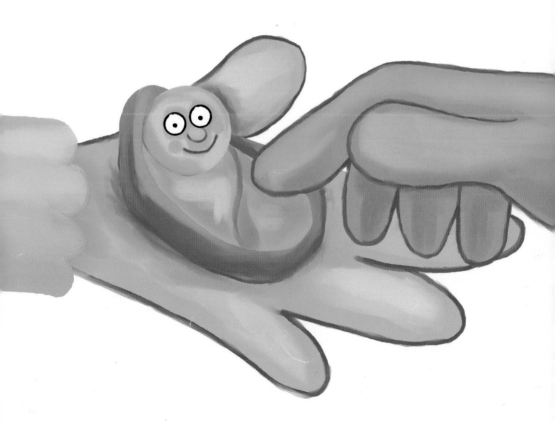

One day, Tom's father went into the forest.

"I'm tired. I wish someone could bring the cart," he said.

"I can!" Tom said.

Tom quickly left to find the horse and the cart. Then he jumped into the horse's ear and began to give commands.

Tom and his cart drove by two men. The men decided to follow the cart.

When Tom found his father, Tom called out
to him.

The woodcutter took his son out of the horse's ear. The strangers were watching.

"We could make a fortune with such a little man," said one stranger.

11

The strangers went to the woodcutter.

"Sell us the little man," one of them said.

Tom whispered to his father, "Take the money. I will escape and be home in time for dinner."

Tom's father sold him to the strangers.

Before long, Tom cried, "Set me down for a moment. I have to do something."

When the stranger put him down, Tom ran into a mouse hole. The strangers could not find him.

At dusk, two thieves walked by.

"How can we get the money?" Tom heard one thief ask.

"I can help you!" Tom said.

The thieves took Tom to the house they wanted to rob.

Tom crawled through the window and yelled, "Do you want all of the money?"

"Yes! And be quiet!" whispered the thieves.

"Whatever you want!" Tom shouted.

At this, the maid woke up. The thieves ran off, and Tom went to the barn to sleep.

The next morning, the maid grabbed a pile of hay for the cows. Tom was sleeping in it. The cow ate the hay and Tom.

"Help!" Tom cried.

The maid was shocked to hear the cow speak. She decided the cow should be butchered.

Tom fell out of the cow. Soon, a hungry wolf came by and ate Tom. But Tom had a plan.

"Dear wolf, I know where you can find a good meal!" he shouted.

Tom described the way to his father's house.

When the wolf arrived at Tom's house, he went into the pantry. After the wolf had eaten, he was so fat, he couldn't get out of the pantry.

Tom screamed as loud as he could. Tom's father and mother ran to the pantry.

Tom yelled, "It's me! Your little Tom! I'm in the wolf's belly. Please get me out."

Tom's parents killed the wolf and saved their son.

"Now that I'm home, I'm never going away again," said Tom.

"And we'll never sell you again," said Tom's father. "Not for all the money in the world."

The End